The Amazing Mushroom Mix–Up

Young Lions
An imprint of HarperCollins Publishers

Have you read

Bats, Boilers and Blackcurrant Jelly
another Araminta Spook book
from HarperCollins

First published in Great Britain in Young Lions in 1994

1 3 5 7 9 10 8 6 4 2

Young Lions is an imprint of HarperCollins Children's Books,
a division of HarperCollins Publishers Ltd,
77-85 Fulham Palace Road, London W6 8JB

Copyright © Angie Sage 1994

ISBN 0 00 674951 8

The author asserts the moral right to be
identified as the author of the work.

Printed and bound in Great Britain
by HarperCollins Manufacturing Ltd, Glasgow

Araminta Spook

THE AMAZING
MUSHROOM MIX-UP

written and illustrated by

Angie Sage

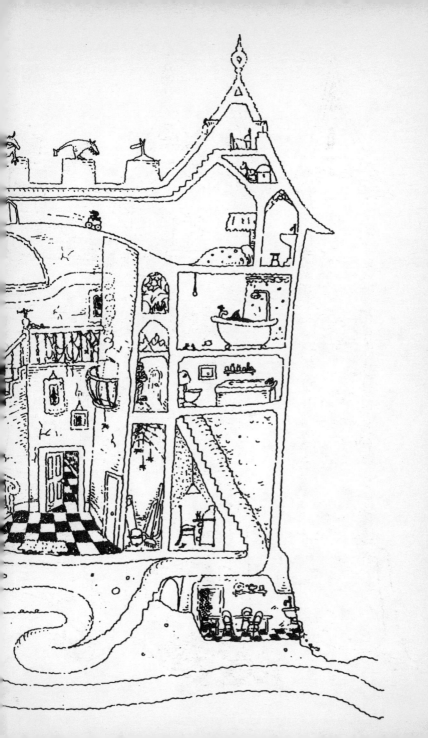

CHAPTER ONE

"We shouldn't be doing this. You know he doesn't like us poking around in his room when he's not there," said Wanda, as she followed Araminta through the secret passage and down the spiral stairs to Sir Horace's room.

"He won't know," said Araminta. "Seeing as he's propped up inside our Monday wardrobe at the moment and won't come out. I don't know what's wrong with the old grump!" She pushed open the door at the bottom of the stairs and stepped into the dusty little room.

"I suppose we might find out why he's in such a bad mood if we had a look around," said Wanda doubtfully. Her torch showed up nothing more than the usual broken chair, old rug, books and candlesticks. Araminta fished out a pile of books from underneath the chair, and a cloud of dust rose into the air making Wanda sneeze.

"I've always wanted to know what was in these books," said Araminta excitedly and she settled down on the floor and carefully opened one of them. Wanda peered over Araminta's shoulder and shone her torch onto the old, yellowing pages. The book was falling to pieces and bits of paper slid out all over the floor. Wanda picked one up:

"Babie's First Year," she read.

"Name Of Babie: Horace Cuthbert Shirley George of The Castile Greene upon the Greene River."

BABIE'S FIRST YEAR ~

Name of Babie
Horace Cuthbert Shirley George
of The Castle Greene upon
the Greene River ~

Horace Cuthbert
aged Foure Monthe

"Shirley!" giggled Wanda. "No wonder he doesn't want us to see these books."

Araminta looked at the piece of paper. There were some drawings of a fat little baby lying on a rug with a few faded words underneath them,

Horace Cuthbert aged Foure Monthe

"Aah, how sweet," said Araminta. "Fancy Sir Horace having been a baby once!"

"Everyone's been a baby once," said Wanda. "Even my dad's been a baby once, although that was ages ago."

"Not as long ago as Sir Horace," said Araminta. "Hey, look at the date, he was born... let's see... four hundred...

um, no... er five hundred and th-forty years ago the day after tomorrow!"

Wanda peered at the date and counted up the years on her fingers.

"Gosh!" she said. "I wonder if Sir Horace ever saw a dinosaur?"

Araminta slammed the book shut in a cloud of dust and leapt to her feet.

"Birthday party!" she said excitedly. "That'll cheer him up. We'll give him a surprise birthday party!"

Araminta and Wanda emerged from the secret passage humming 'Happy Birthday to You' and wandered up to the Monday bedroom (Araminta and Wanda shared a different bedroom on each day of the week).

A muffled voice came from the wardrobe. "What are you humming that for?" asked the armour-clad ghost.

"You'll be five hundred and forty the day after tomorr..." Araminta kicked Wanda, "...OW!"

"We're not meant to know that, you wally," hissed Araminta.

"No I won't be," said the voice. "I'll only be five hundred and thirty nine. Now go away and leave me alone."

"All right, Sir Horace, we'll go away and forget all about it!" Araminta said brightly and she dragged Wanda out of the bedroom.

"Aren't we going to have a party, then?" Wanda sounded disappointed.

"'Course we are, silly," said Araminta. "But this time you keep quiet about it, OK? Now let's go and see Brenda about the food."

CHAPTER TWO

Brenda was down in the boiler room polishing the boiler and quietly singing to it when Araminta and Wanda burst in.

"Hi Mum!" yelled Wanda.

"Ooooh!" squeaked Nigel, and he melted back through the wall into the secret passage behind it.

Nigel was a small and rather timid ghost who had started to visit Brenda while she looked after the boiler.

Araminta's Great Aunt Tabitha used to look after the boiler. She also used to shout at it, kick it and throw the coal scuttle around. In fact she used to make so much noise that Nigel had thought that a huge monster with six arms and lots of very big feet lived in the boiler room.

Things had become much quieter ever since Wanda, her mum, Brenda Wizzard and her dad, Barry Wizzard, had moved in to share the house with Araminta Spook, Gertrude the Guinea Pig, Great Aunt Tabitha Spook and Great Uncle Drac Spook. Barry could do strange spells and was teaching Wanda some of them.

"And how are the two terrors today?" asked Brenda, smiling as she brushed the final speck of soot from one of the air vents of her beloved boiler. "What are you two up to now?"

"Mu-um," said Wanda. "Can we have some crisps and things?"

"Planning a midnight feast?" asked her mum. "Go on then, but leave me a few of those nice eel 'n' onion ones."

Brenda stood up and patted the boiler. "You know," she said, "that Nigel has some interesting stories to tell. He says that the secret passage he lives in leads to a tunnel. He says that's how poor old Sir Horace got here: he was chased out of his castle by marauding hordes..."

"What's a Marauding Horde, Mum?" asked Wanda.

"Um, I think it's a sort of wild horde, dear. Anyway this horde thing chased him, but something awful happened to him on the way and he got stuck somewhere horrible, but Nigel wouldn't say much about that. Then Sir Horace came along the tunnel and found himself here. He's never dared go back again."

"Does he want to go back then?" asked Wanda thoughtfully.

"Well, Nigel thought that Sir Horace

often gets homesick and that's why he sometimes goes and sits in his room."

"Or in our wardrobe," said Araminta. "That's probably why he's there now!"

Araminta and Wanda were in Brenda's crisp-store when they heard a loud THUMPPP! It seemed to come from Great Uncle Drac's turret. Great Uncle Drac kept hundreds of bats in the turret at the side of the house, and he slept there all day in a sleeping bag which hung from the rafters at the very top of the turret. At the bottom was a large bat-flap

It was towards this bat-flap that
Brenda, Araminta and Wanda raced
when they heard the thump.

Great Aunt Tabitha had got there
first and was already squeezing through.
Araminta and Wanda followed her but
Brenda only got halfway.

"I'm stuck!"

Inside the turret a lumpy sleeping
bag was lying on the ground, or, more
exactly, on half a metre of bat
droppings, surrounded by a cloud of
flapping, worried bats. Great Aunt
Tabitha and Araminta pushed their
way through.

"Drac, Drac, are you all right?"
cried Great Aunt Tabitha.

"Eeuurgh, I fell... my legs..."
moaned Great Uncle Drac.

"Quick! Get Barry! We'll take him to hospital in Barry's van," said Great Aunt Tabitha.

"Aaargh..." moaned Great Uncle Drac.

"It's all right, Drac dear," Great Aunt Tabitha was saying, then "Where's Barry?" she yelled.

"Here I am," came a voice from behind Brenda.

"I'm very sorry," said Brenda from the bat-flap, "but I seem to be a little bit stuck."

"How are we going to get out, Aunt Tabby?" said Araminta. "How are we going to get Uncle Drac to hospital?"

"Dad!" yelled Wanda as she fought off a frightened bat. "This is an emergency! Do something!"

"I'll try," came Barry's muffled voice.

There was a loud popping noise, a blue flash, and Brenda was suddenly sitting on the boiler looking dazed.

"Oooh!" said Brenda. "That's hot!"

"Sorry, dear! I didn't mean you to

end up there," said Barry.

"I'll... um... I'll go and get the van," said Brenda, and she wandered off rather unsteadily.

Much later, when it was dark, they all came back from the hospital. Great Uncle Drac had both his legs in plaster and was not in a good mood. He took up residence in the broom cupboard by the front door, sitting in a large chair with both his legs stuck out in front of him. He held a pair of knitting needles, a ball of green wool and a book called, *How To Knit Your First Scarf* which was a

get-well-present from Great Aunt
Tabitha.

"What about my bats?" he moaned.
"No one's fed my bats and look at the
time! My delivery to the mushroom farm
is late already. I should have been there
half an hour ago. Whatever's going to
happen to Drac's Organic Bat Fertilisers?"

"Don't you worry, Drac dear,"
said Brenda. "Barry will do it, won't
you Barry?"

"What?" said Barry.

"You'll look after Drac's bats won't
you, dear?" Brenda turned to Great
Uncle Drac. "He won't mind feeding
your bats and shovelling up the bat-poo
every night and taking it down to the
mushroom farm. You'll do it, won't you
Barry... Barry?"

CHAPTER THREE

The next morning Barry was arguing with Great Uncle Drac.

"I really don't see why you're making such a fuss, and I still don't see why you have to deliver this... stuff... at night. It makes much more sense to take it first thing in the morning."

"They were expecting it last night," grumbled Great Uncle Drac. "I always deliver it at night, I've been doing it for years. That's when the mushrooms like it."

"How can you possibly know what mushrooms like?" asked Barry tetchily.

"I understand mushrooms," said Great Uncle Drac. "Me and mushrooms have a lot in common, we both like the dark and peace and quiet. Now go away, close the door and leave me alone."

Barry went away in a bad mood. He bumped into Araminta who was trying to ride Wanda's bike, or more exactly, Araminta bumped into him.

"Right, you two," he said. "You can come and make yourselves useful!"

Five bulging sacks of bat droppings later, Araminta said to Wanda, "You can hold the umbrella now if you like, and I'll do some shovelling."

"Oh, thank you so much," said Wanda, somewhat crossly Araminta thought, as she scraped up the last bit and shovelled it into a sack, "but Dad and I have finished now."

"Well at least my umbrella kept the bat-poo off you both. There's a lot of it coming down with all those bats flying around and if I hadn't stood here for hours holding it, you and Barry would not be nice to know."

Wanda did not answer. She dragged

a heavy sack towards the bat flap and heaved it through. Araminta grabbed the next one. "Here, let me help," she said.

"Don't strain yourself," mumbled Wanda.

"OK, I'll wait outside for you then." Araminta wandered off upstairs and sat on the front doorstep in the sunshine.

"Minty... is that you?" A voice drifted out from the broom cupboard.

Araminta poked her head around the cupboard door and peered into the gloom. The only light came from a small flickering candle that Great Aunt Tabitha had insisted on putting there after she had tripped over Great Uncle Drac's legs for the fourth time.

Araminta could see two white things hovering about a foot above the ground and for a moment she thought that she had discovered two crocodile ghosts.

How nice she decided, Nigel and Sir Horace could have one each as pets. Then she realised that they were Great Uncle Drac's legs in plaster resting on the footstool.

"Hello, Uncle Drac," said Araminta.

"Minty," Great Uncle Drac sounded sorry for himself. "Minty, what's that Barry doing? Hasn't he gone to the mushroom farm yet?"

"We're just going, Uncle Drac, he's putting the sacks in the van then we'll be off."

"How many sacks did you get?"

"Um, five I think."

"Not bad, not bad, considering the shock they had when I fell."

"Oh, Uncle Drac, how are you feeling?" Araminta gave him a big hug.

"Better when Barry starts taking the bat business seriously."

"He is, really he is. Now don't you worry." Araminta heard the engine of Barry's van start. "See you later!"

Araminta rushed out just as the van

was beginning to move off.

"Hey, wait for me!" she yelled.

Wanda wound down the window. "I got the front seat, you'll have to sit in the back with the sacks."

Araminta stomped round to the back of the van, opened the doors, squeezed herself in and banged the doors shut again. Her nose tried to tell her something. "Eurgh... phewwooff!"

But it was too late to get out. Barry's van was speeding along the lane on the way to the mushroom farm.

CHAPTER FOUR

Two long traffic jams and a very bumpy ride later, Barry's van drove through the gates of the Miracle Mushroom Farm. Barry opened the van doors and Araminta fell out.

"Fresh air, give me fresh air," she gasped. Barry and Wanda pulled out the sacks.

"I'll go and find Morris Miracle and explain why these are a bit late," he said. "You look as though you could do

with some exercise, Araminta. Why don't you two go and have a run around on Castle Green over there." Barry pointed to a grassy mound with some rocks sticking out of it.

"Don't go near the river," he said.

"We won't, Dad," said Wanda.

"Great!" Araminta grabbed hold of Wanda's hand and dragged her off.

After rolling down the grassy banks and climbing over all the rocks, Araminta and Wanda sat in the sunshine. Araminta picked up a handful of small stones and threw them one by one on to a flat piece of rock.

"Ten!" she said. "Bet you can't get ten on there in one go."

Wanda was not a good shot and most of the stones missed. Her last

27

throw was with a big round stone that she had doodled 'Wanda Wizz' on. She threw it carefully and it hit the rock but bounced straight off and disappeared. Plink... plonk... plunk. The stone fell down somewhere far below them.

"Did you hear that?" Wanda said to Araminta. "It sounded just like a marble falling in your marble maze."

"But it doesn't count," said Araminta, "because it didn't stay on."

"So what. Where do you think it's gone? It dropped into something, didn't it?" asked Wanda.

She went over to where the stone had disappeared and found a small gap in the rock. "I wish I had my torch," she said.

Araminta got up and sauntered over.

"You could borrow mine," she said casually. "I always carry one – you never know when you might need one."

Wanda took Araminta's torch and shone it down into the gap.

"Wow," she breathed. "Look at that!"

Araminta looked down along the narrow torchbeam and saw a small chamber far below them. It seemed to have a mosaic floor with swords and spears scattered over it.

"Phew..." she whistled.

"Do you know where I think we are?" asked Wanda. "I think we are right above the remains of the castle that Sir Horace came from. You know, the Castile Greene."

"Castile Greene... Castle Green... I suppose it could be," said Araminta thoughtfully.

"It's got to be! Look, there's even a river here, that must be the River Greene." Wanda stood up excitedly.

"I've got a really great idea. This," she announced, pointing to the small gap in the rock, "is where we have Sir Horace's five hundred and fortieth birthday party!"

"What, on that rock?" asked Araminta. "There's not much space."

"No, not on the rock, silly. Down there, in that chamber down inside the castle!" Wanda folded her arms and looked pleased.

"You're joking," said Araminta. "How are we going to get in there? We can't squeeze through this gap."

"Easy," said Wanda. "You remember what my mum said this morning. All we have to do is go along the secret tunnel and I bet we'll end up here. Just think what a great place it would be to have Sir Horace's party. He'd love it."

"I suppose it might get him out of

our wardrobe... we could think about it," said Araminta.

They were still thinking when Barry called them and they ran back to the van to find Barry loading the sacks of bat-poo back in again. He looked really grumpy.

"What are you doing, Dad?" asked Wanda.

Barry heaved in the last sack and said between gritted teeth, "Mr Mingey Morris Miracle Mushroom has cancelled the order, so I'm taking it all back, that's what I'm doing!"

"Oh no!" Araminta and Wanda said together.

"What will Uncle Drac say?" asked Araminta.

"Quite a lot, I expect," said Barry glumly.

They all got silently into the van. Wanda let Araminta share the front seat.

Barry drove slowly along the winding lanes.

"The thing is," he said. "Morris Miracle didn't cancel the order because it arrived this morning instead of last night, he actually said it was better to have it in the morning and he never liked having to wait up until midnight for Drac to arrive."

"Why *did* he cancel it then, Dad?" asked Wanda.

"He cancelled it because he's not growing organic mushrooms anymore and he's using chemical fertiliser now as it's so much cheaper."

"Yuk!" said Wanda.

"But that's not the worst thing," said Barry. "He's been using the chemicals for ages but he was too scared of Drac to tell him that he didn't want his organic bat-poo anymore. He's just been buying it off him and chucking it into a hole in the ground. Of course when he saw me and heard that Drac was out of action for months –"

"He told you to tell Uncle Drac," finished Araminta.

"That's all right then, Dad," said Wanda. "It's not your fault."

"Do you think Drac will believe that?" asked Barry.

"No," said Araminta and Wanda together.

They drove along in silence for a while, then Barry said, "I can't tell Drac yet."

"You'll have to tell him some time, Dad," said Wanda.

"Later," said Barry, "later, when he's feeling a bit better."

"You mean when you're feeling a bit better," said Wanda.

When they got home Barry parked the van around the back and put the sacks into an old shed at the bottom of the garden.

Wanda looked at Araminta.

"Well," she said. "What about this party in the castle, then?"

"OK," said Araminta. "Let's go and get some crisps and coke and torches and a compass and string and…"

"String? What do we want string for?" asked Wanda.

"So that we can find our way back again," explained Araminta.

"We can use Dad's garden string," said Wanda. "I'll go and get it."

"I'll go and get the crisps and coke, and I'll see you in ten minutes by the attic stairs."

CHAPTER FIVE

It was nearly lunchtime. Down in the third kitchen on the right just past the boiler room, Barry was peeling a huge pile of potatoes. Great Uncle Drac was asleep at last in the broom cupboard. Asleep at last after Great Aunt Tabitha had found his sleeping bag, helped him into it, refused to hang it from the ceiling on account of the doctor having told him to keep his feet up, found his knitting and finally collected some of the more house-trained bats to keep him company.

Great Aunt Tabitha had quietly tiptoed out when: "Tabby... can I have a drink of water?" drifted plaintively from under the broom cupboard door. Great Uncle Drac was awake again.

One drink of water later, Great Aunt Tabitha had gone upstairs to inspect her new project. She thought she saw Araminta and Wanda scuttle off and disappear through a wall. "Must get some new glasses," she mumbled to herself.

Great Aunt Tabitha picked up her hammer and looked at the 250cc Triumph motorbike engine that she had begun to take apart, scattering bits of it all over the lino in bathroom number two. There were at least six bathrooms in the house and Great Aunt Tabitha used bathroom number two because no one else did. No one had dared have a bath in there for years, due to the

old story that the bath was haunted by piranha fish.

Great Aunt Tabitha happily set about banging away, trying to remove the flywheel which was rusted onto the crankshaft. The noise echoed around the bathroom, BANG! CLANG! PRANG! .... OUCH!!!! and filled the house.

"Funny," said Barry to Brenda, as he broke another egg into a large mixing jug, "how Tabitha always manages to find something noisy to do."

Brenda thoughtfully stroked Pusskins, her cat, "Can you hear someone shouting or is it just my ears ringing?"

"Probably just your ears," said Barry. "Pass the salt, could you?"

"Tabithaaa... Oi, TabithAAAA!" Great Uncle Drac was yelling up in the broom cupboard. "Where's my green wool? WHERE'S MY GREEN WOOL?!"

Great Uncle Drac could not get to sleep, so he had picked up his knitting only to find that the wool had disappeared, and

as far as he could make out everyone else had disappeared too.

"Oi, Big Bat," he said to a big bat. "Go and fetch my green wool."

The bat sat and stared at him with small, half-closed, batty eyes. Great Uncle Drac coughed politely.

"Please could you go and fetch my green wool, Big Bat, if you wouldn't mind."

Big Bat opened the door and flew off. He had no idea where to find any green wool and only a very hazy idea about what green wool might be. It was not something that his mum, Bertha Bat, had taught him about.

"Bother this for a lark," Big Bat was thinking, when he suddenly saw what looked to him like a piece of green wool sticking out from underneath a wall and tied to the attic stairs. Bertha Bat had taught Big Bat about knots and he quickly untied it and began to pull. It became longer and longer.

"Just the ticket," muttered Big Bat to himself and he took the end of the green 'wool' down to Great Uncle Drac in the broom cupboard.

"It's a bit thick and hairy," he said ungratefully.

Big Bat stared at him and bared his teeth. "But, er, thank you all the same, Big Bat," muttered Great Uncle Drac, and he got on with knitting a very thick and hairy green scarf.

"LUNCHTIME!" yelled Barry from the basement.

Great Aunt Tabitha always heard words like 'lunchtime', 'breakfast' and 'cup of tea?'. She put down her hammer and went downstairs, nearly tripping over a piece of green string that was trailing out from under the attic stairs and slowly moving down through the house and into the broom cupboard.

"I don't know what those two are up to now," said Great Aunt Tabitha to Brenda in the kitchen. "They seem to be playing some strange string game with Drac."

"We'll soon find out," said Brenda.

"WandAAA.... AramintAAAA.... lu-UNCH!"

"That's funny," said Great Aunt Tabitha five minutes later. "They're never usually late for lunch. I'll go and see what they're up to."

She returned looking puzzled. "They're not with Drac, and I haven't seen them since you got back from

Miracle Mushrooms."

"Come to think of it, neither have we," said Barry and Brenda.

"Hmmm... although I did wonder if I saw them not long ago..." said Great Aunt Tabitha thoughtfully. "I think something's going on."

CHAPTER SIX

Something was going on.

In a maze of dark, damp tunnels far beyond the house, Araminta was saying to Wanda, "I don't think my compass is working properly anymore, we just seem to be going round and round in circles."

"It was all right until we got to that funny portcullis thing," said Wanda as they arrived at yet another fork in the tunnel. She shone the torch along the

two tunnels. One sloped up and turned
left, one sloped down and turned right.

"It's your turn to choose," she said
to Araminta.

"Um, the one that goes... up."

They set off along Araminta's tunnel
but as soon as they had turned the
corner they found some steps going
down straight ahead of them and a
tunnel on each side of them.

"Your turn," said Araminta.

"Oh... let's try the steps," said Wanda.

They went down the steps, around
two corners and straight into a brick
wall. It was a dead end.

"Not again!" said Wanda.

Wanda and Araminta were beginning to get tired. They had come a long way since Wanda had done her 'sleep spell' on Nigel, the guardian of the tunnel, so that they could both walk through him and into the maze.

At first it was easy, they just followed the tunnel away from the house. Wanda had worked out that Castle Green was north west, and sure enough that was the direction that the tunnel took. It had taken them up and down gentle slopes, over underground streams and through rooms with weapons scattered all around and suits of armour rusting in heaps. It had run on and on, always going north west.

Until, that is, they reached a rusty old portcullis that blocked their path.

"That," Araminta said, "must be the entrance to the castle. All castles have portcullises."

"Port-whats?" said Wanda.

"Portcullises, gate thingies like this rusty old thing here. They open like this.'

Araminta grabbed a chain that was wrapped around a pulley and pulled hard. The portcullis rose up, creaking and clanking as it went and they rushed underneath it, seconds before it slammed down behind them. They were then faced with a long, damp flight of steps that took them down and down and down and at the bottom of which was a maze of tunnels. Now they had reached another dead end.

"OK," said Araminta. "Let's try and get back to the bottom of the steps and start again. There must be an easy way out of this. Pass us the string."

"You've already got the string," said Wanda.

"No I haven't," said Araminta. "You've got it."

"No I haven't," said Wanda.

"Stop joking, Wanda, that's not funny," said Araminta crossly.

"I'm not joking..." said Wanda.

"What?"

"I'm not joking. I haven't got it. You had it last."

"No I didn't."

"Yes you did."

"Didn't!"

"Did!"

There was silence, as Araminta and Wanda looked at each other in horror, "Oh no!" they wailed. "We're lost! Where's the string gone?"

At that moment most of it was in Great Uncle Drac's broom cupboard turning into an unusually thick and hairy scarf.

CHAPTER SEVEN

After lunch Great Aunt Tabitha went back upstairs to see Great Uncle Drac.

"Drac, are you sure you haven't seen Araminta and Wanda?" she asked, then she peered more closely at the scarf. "Goodness, Drac, your knitting is... well... amazing. What's it going to be?"

"It's a scarf, Tabitha, you know, like the one in the book you gave me. Can't you tell?" Great Uncle Drac sounded hurt.

Suddenly the door to the broom cupboard burst open.

"Hey!" said Barry, "What are you doing with my best garden string? It's running all over the house! I was just about to tie the beans up with it."

Great Uncle Drac looked cross, it was getting far too crowded in the broom cupboard for his liking.

"What string?" he snapped.

Barry looked at the scarf. Then he looked at his string which was slowly running into the broom cupboard, up over the arm of Great Uncle Drac's chair, winding round his knitting kneedles and turning into a scarf.

Barry looked at Great Aunt Tabitha.

"That doctor at the hospital, did she say anything about him having hit his head?" he asked.

Great Uncle Drac put his knitting down.

"That's it!" he said. "I've had enough! First you're rude about my lovely scarf and now you're going on about my head. You can all just GO AWAY!"

Great Uncle Drac blew out the candle and put his sleeping bag over his head.

"It's going crazy in here," said Barry. "I need some fresh air."

Barry went off to the shed at the bottom of the garden where he had been hiding the sacks of bat droppings. He had been worrying about what to do with them. He knew that every day there would be more to hide and the shed was very small.

Inside the shed, Barry started digging a large, deep hole.

Back inside the house, Great Aunt Tabitha was looking at the string. "This has to be something to do with Araminta and Wanda..." she thought.

Great Aunt Tabitha started to follow it. She went up the big dusty staircase.

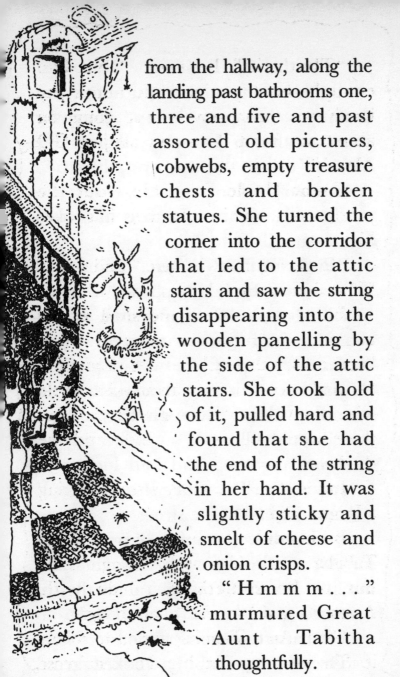

from the hallway, along the landing past bathrooms one, three and five and past assorted old pictures, cobwebs, empty treasure chests and broken statues. She turned the corner into the corridor that led to the attic stairs and saw the string disappearing into the wooden panelling by the side of the attic stairs. She took hold of it, pulled hard and found that she had the end of the string in her hand. It was slightly sticky and smelt of cheese and onion crisps.

"H m m m . . ." murmured Great Aunt Tabitha thoughtfully.

"Tabitha! Oh Tabitha!"

Brenda came pounding up the stairs, thumpety thumpety thump, along the corridor, thump thumpety, around the corner, crash thump, and thumped down onto the floor.

"Brenda, what on earth is it?" asked Great Aunt Tabitha.

"Puff... Puff! It's Nigel... he just said that... something odd happened to him... he fell asleep on the floor and he dreamt that he had been run over by a steamroller... puff... now he thinks it might have been Araminta and Wanda walking through him to get into the tunnel!"

Brenda got up and and looked at Great Aunt Tabitha who was still holding the end of the string.

"What have you got Barry's string for? Do you think it was Araminta and my little Wanda? You don't think they've gone along the tunnel to the Castle, do you? What are we going to do?

Great Aunt Tabitha looked grim.

"I've got Barry's string," she said, "because I think Araminta has used it as her exploring string. Yes, I do think it was Araminta and your little Wanda and yes, I do think they have gone along the tunnel to the Castle. What we are going to do is go after them before they get into trouble."

"Perhaps I ought to make some sandwiches first," said Brenda, who was not at all sure about going down a tunnel. In her experience, tunnels were nasty narrow things that you got stuck in.

Great Aunt Tabitha took no notice. She rummaged around in one of her deep pockets and brought out a large rusty key, and from another pocket she produced a torch. She put the key in what looked to Brenda like a hole in the

panelling under the attic stairs, turned it, and a small door swung silently open.

Brenda looked doubtfully into the gloom. "I could just go and make a flask of tea," she said. "It looks cold in there."

Great Aunt Tabitha pushed her in and the door closed behind them.

"Brenda," said Great Aunt Tabitha firmly, "there is no time to lose!"

Brenda was not at all happy at being in a small, secret passage but she followed Great Aunt Tabitha down the spiral stairs, through Sir Horace's room and down the steep steps to where the passage ran behind the boiler room.

Nigel saw them. Brenda thought he looked rather sheepish.

"Nigel!" boomed Great Aunt Tabitha, her voice echoing around the passageway. "What is the reason for you being here?"

Nigel hovered very nervously just above the floor. He looked pale, even for a ghost.

"To be the guard ghost and at all

times to protect the house from the Castle and the Castle from the house." he recited.

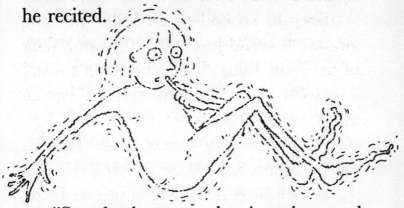

"So why have you let Araminta and Wanda go past you?"

"I... I was asleep..." Nigel faltered. "I saw some stars and fell asleep... I'm sorry, it's never happened before... I'm still feeling a bit... strange."

"What colour stars?" asked Brenda.

"Um, purple... er... with pink edges."

"Sleep stars!" said Brenda. "I told Barry that Wanda was too young to learn the sleep spell, but would he listen to me?"

"Come on Brenda," said Great Aunt Tabitha. "We must find Araminta and Wanda before –"

"Before what?" asked Brenda.

Great Aunt Tabitha turned to Brenda and looked at her seriously.

"Look Brenda, I don't want to worry you, but at the end of this tunnel there is a water maze that guards the entrance to the castle. The river rises at high tide and floods into the lower half of the maze. That's what happened to Sir Horace all those years ago."

"But Sir Horace is a ghost," said Brenda.

"He wasn't a ghost before he got stuck in the maze at high tide," answered Great Aunt Tabitha quietly.

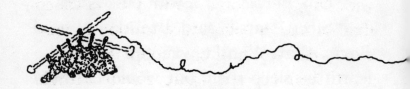

CHAPTER EIGHT

Barry threw the spade out of the hole and clambered up after it. He was pleased with his afternoon's work. He reckoned that he had enough space to hide at least two weeks' worth of bat droppings.

"Then I'll tell Drac about Morris Miracle," he thought.

It was beginning to get dark as Barry came back into the house and kicked off his muddy boots.

Great Uncle Drac was wide awake.

"Barry?" he called out. "Is that you?"

Barry poked his head around the door of the broom cupboard.

"Er, hello Drac. All right, are you? Had a nice sleep?"

"Not bad. Where's my cup of tea? Is everyone deaf around here?"

Barry had spent the afternoon telling himself that he had to be nice to Great Uncle Drac because he did have two broken legs, so he said, "Sorry Drac, have they been ignoring you? I'll go and make you a nice cup of tea now."

Barry set off down to the second kitchen on the left just before the boiler room. There was no one around. Barry turned on the lights and Pusskins rushed up to him complaining loudly.

"Where is everyone, Pusskins?" said Barry, picking her up.

He lit the gas and put the kettle on, then stood in the empty kitchen and realised that something was very strange. The house was silent.

Barry made the tea and took a cup upstairs to Great Uncle Drac.

"It's very quiet, Drac," said Barry. "Where's everyone gone?"

Great Uncle Drac grunted.

"I expect they've gone out so that I could get some sleep. It's about time I had a bit of peace and quiet. This tea's too strong."

"You... I'll go and make another cup for you, Drac."

Barry looked at the hall clock. He had never noticed what a loud tick-tock sound it made before. It was nearly supper time and it was Brenda's

turn to cook. Brenda usually spent hours getting supper ready and there was no sign of her anywhere. Barry began to feel worried.

Barry shivered. It was getting cold and he went to check the boiler. It was nearly out so he shook the ashes out and put some more coal in. Now he was really worried; Brenda never let the boiler die down like that.

"Barry..." came a small ghostly voice.

"Aaaargh!" yelled Barry and dropped the coal scuttle on his foot. "Ow!"

It was Nigel.

Barry had not met Nigel before but he had heard about him from Brenda. Although Barry knew all about spells he knew nothing about ghosts and he stepped back and tried to feel brave.

Nigel hovered and coughed politely. "I...

um, I think I should tell you... I've had a bit of a bad day."

"So have I," said Barry.

Nigel shuffled about.

"No, er... what I mean is that I've let four people through to the tunnel and I've never done that before in my life – well, I don't mean in my life exactly, I mean I've never done that before, ever, honestly. You see, the first two threw these stars all over me and then the next two, well that tall thin noisy one, you know the Tabitha one, she said she'd put me in the boiler and so I had to let them through, didn't I?"

"What," said Barry, "are you going on about?"

"They haven't come back," said Nigel, "and it's high tide in a few hours."

"Who hasn't come back?" asked Barry slowly, but he knew what Nigel was going to say.

"Araminta, Wanda, Tabitha and my friend Brenda."

"I was afraid you might say that," said Barry.

CHAPTER NINE

"What do you think that noise is?" Araminta asked Wanda.

They were sitting miserably on a pile of stones in a small cavern. It was the first place they had found where they could sit down. They were tired and had decided to rest for a while and think about what to do next.

"It sounds like water to me," said Wanda.

"I haven't heard that before," said Araminta. "Have you?"

"No," said Wanda. They were both quiet.

"How far from the river are we?" asked Araminta.

Wanda shivered. "How should I know?"

"Look," said Araminta. "We must be underneath the castle now. How far is the castle from the river?"

"Not far," said Wanda, her teeth chattering.

"How far does the river come up at high tide?" persisted Araminta.

"Oh shut up about the river," snapped Wanda. "I don't want to think about it."

Araminta got up and shone her torch along to the end of the cavern. The torchlight bounced off dark, lapping water.

Araminta pulled Wanda to her feet, "Come on," she said. "We've got to get out of here."

They walked back to the tunnel that

they had just come through, but had only walked a few metres when Araminta felt her feet getting wet.

"W-Wanda," she said. "Look!" She shone the torch down at her feet and they both looked at the water which was slowly creeping towards them in gentle rocking movements.

"We could paddle through it and get to a dry bit," said Wanda.

"But the tunnel goes *down*, so it can only get deeper," said Araminta, trying not to panic.

"Oh," said Wanda.

They knew that they were trapped. Both ways out of the cavern were full of rising water.

Wanda looked sick. "We'll just have to go back to the pile of stones and hope that it doesn't get any higher," she said.

They walked back to the stone pile and sat down again. Wanda sat and stared at the floor, while Araminta listened to the water. She could hear it creeping closer and closer towards them, making its little lapping sounds. The air around them got colder as the water got closer. Araminta stared at the water, willing it to go down again,

"It *has* to be high tide now, it just has to be! It can't get any higher. Go down, go down, go DOWN!"

But the water crept up... and up... and up.

"Hey," said Wanda suddenly. "Look!" She leapt up and picked up a small stone. "Give me the torch, quick!" she cried, grabbing it from Araminta.

Written clearly on the stone were the words WANDA WIZZ.

"That's my stone!" said Wanda excitedly. "You know, the one that disappeared when we were on Castle Green."

"But I thought it landed in that room with all the swords in," said Araminta.

"It must have dropped through," said Wanda. "We must be just below the sword room. If we could get up there we'd be safe."

Wanda shone the torch along the brickwork roof of the cavern and the torchlight picked out a jagged hole and shone up through it, out of the cavern and up into the chamber.

Wanda stepped back excitedly and cold water ran over her socks. She gasped. "Quick, we've got to pile these stones up higher and try to reach the roof!"

They scrabbled at the stones and made a tall thin pile. Wanda climbed carefully up and stood on tiptoe and stretched her arms up to reach the hole in the roof. "I... I can't reach!"

"Let me try," said Araminta, who was now standing on the pile of stones anyway, trying to keep her feet dry. "I'm taller than you."

Wanda came down and helped Araminta up to the top of the stones.

"I can just about get hold of the edges..." puffed Araminta. She stretched herself as tall as she possibly could but the stone she was standing on rocked and bricks began to fall from the roof above her.

"Ooo-oh!" Araminta lost her balance, and the whole pile of stones moved from under her feet and tumbled down into the water, closely followed by Araminta and Wanda.

CHAPTER TEN

Just as Araminta and Wanda were falling off the pile of stones, Great Aunt Tabitha and Brenda were arriving at the portcullis.

Great Aunt Tabitha pulled hard on the chain just as Araminta had done and it rose slowly up again. They walked through and Great Aunt Tabitha wound it back down.

Brenda and Great Aunt Tabitha

looked at the steep flight of steps disappearing before them. A dank smell of the river drifted up towards them.

"What's the time, Brenda?" asked Great Aunt Tabitha.

"Well, it must be well past supper time; I'm starving." Brenda looked at her watch which hung around her neck. "Oh, it's half past six."

"It will be high tide in an hour then," said Great Aunt Tabitha. "We had better get a move on."

Brenda went very pale. "You don't really think they've gone down there? My poor little Wanda can't swim."

"Neither can Araminta," said Great Aunt Tabitha. "But swimming isn't going to do them much good in a tunnel full of water, is it?"

"Oh, don't!" gasped Brenda and hurried down the steps behind Great Aunt Tabitha.

"Drac! Drac!"

Great Uncle Drac stirred irritably. He had dropped off to sleep again while he was waiting for Barry to bring him another cup of tea.

"GerrrOFF!" Drac mumbled, half dreaming that Big Bat was pushing him over a cliff.

"DRAC!" yelled Barry, shaking him again.

Great Uncle Drac woke up with a start.

"What... Oh! You got my tea then, Barry?"

"No, I haven't got your tea," snapped Barry. "There's something wrong."

"Has that teapot broken again?"

"What teapot? Look Drac, this is important, I've got someone to see you." Barry put his head around the door of the broom cupboard and spoke to someone outside in the hallway, "It's all right, you can come in now."

Great Uncle Drac sat up, "Who's that... Oh my goodness! Oh, good afternoon Sir Horace, um, do have a seat. Barry, get those bats off the chair, would you?"

Sir Horace shuffled in and propped himself up against the wall.

"I'd rather stand, if you don't mind, Drac. Not a lot of time, eh Barry?"

"That's right, Sir Horace."

"What's going on?" Great Uncle Drac blinked at Sir Horace and Barry standing squashed up inside the broom cupboard. He had a strange feeling that he might still be dreaming.

"Right," said Barry, "it's like this, Drac: I was down in the kitchen wondering where everyone had got to when I met that little ghost, you know, Nigel. He told me that first Araminta and Wanda, then Brenda and Tabitha had gone past him along the tunnel to the Castle."

"What! He's not meant to let anyone through." Great Uncle Drac looked cross.

"He knows that, Drac, but he couldn't help it. The thing is, they haven't come back and Nigel says that when he woke up he saw the end of Araminta's green string going back past him towards the house."

"What's all this about green string? First it was *your* green string, now it's *Araminta's* green string."

"And now it's *your* green string." Barry pointed at the half-finished scarf that Great Uncle Drac had thrown onto the floor.

"You have been knitting a scarf out of the string Araminta and Wanda were going to use to find their way back again."

"What?" Great Uncle Drac was

becoming very confused.

"That means," said Barry, trying to be patient, "that Araminta and Wanda are probably lost. Tabitha and Brenda may be lost too. Anyway, Nigel told me that I had to find Sir Horace, and that took ages."

Sir Horace shuffled uncomfortably,

"'Don't usually sit in the wardrobe. Sorry about that."

Barry looked at Great Uncle Drac. "Sir Horace told me about the water maze. It's high tide soon."

"Oh," said Great Uncle Drac quietly. "I hadn't thought about that."

"Right!" boomed Sir Horace. "You get the picture, Drac. Bit of a crisis. Don't panic! Got stuck in the maze meself once, not a lot of fun. High tide and all that, terrible rust ever since. Can't let Araminta and Wanda get rusty, what?"

"So," said Barry. "It's no good going along the tunnel from the house, we'll never get there in time. I'm going to take Sir Horace in the van to find the entrance to the escape tunnel that leads into the maze; he's got an old map of the maze."

Barry held out his arm to Sir Horace. "All right, Sir Horace? Time we were off I think."

Sir Horace pushed himself forwards and began to rattle out of the door.

"Hey, what about me?" asked Great Uncle Drac plaintively.

Barry looked flustered. "You'll have to stay here, Drac. You know you can't go anywhere with those legs in plaster. We've got to hurry."

"You can't leave me here alone," said Great Uncle Drac.

"I thought you liked being alone," said Barry, as he steered Sir Horace towards the front door.

"Supposing you all get lost in the maze," said Great Uncle Drac. "I'd just be stuck here for ever and ever."

"No!" said Barry firmly. "We've got to hurry. 'Bye."

"Barry!"

"WHAT?"

"Please..."

So Barry brought the van around to the front of the house where he managed to get most of Sir Horace into the front seat.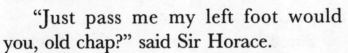

"Just pass me my left foot would you, old chap?" said Sir Horace.

"Here you are, Sir Horace," said Barry, picking a rusty pointed foot off the ground, then spotting a large bolt, "Oh, is this yours?"

"Thanks, old chap, I think that might have fallen off my elbow. No! Ah, it seems to fit on your door, just here."

Then Barry opened the back of the van and heaved Great Uncle Drac in with a pile of cushions and blankets.

"Phew! You sort yourself out, Drac, we've got to rush."

Barry started up the van and they rattled and thumped along the road towards Castle Green.

CHAPTER ELEVEN

It was nearly seven o'clock.

Araminta and Wanda had managed to rebuild the pile of stones and were now sitting at the top of it. Their feet were in the water.

"Want a crisp?" asked Araminta.

"No thanks, they're all soggy now," said Wanda, who was busy shining the torch up at the roof of the cavern.

"I'm sure we could get up there,"

she said, "if I stood on your shoulders..."

"We would both end up in the water again," said Araminta glumly. "It's not worth the risk, is it? Look how deep it is now."

They both looked down towards the swirling pool that surrounded them. The water was rising fast and flowing swiftly along the cavern and through into the tunnel. Araminta and Wanda could barely see the roof of the tunnel now.

Araminta sniffed. "I wonder if Gertrude is missing me? She won't have had her tea."

"Lucky old Gertrude," said Wanda. "I wish it was me in a nice, dry ballroom with my mice." She looked at the dark water and shivered. "Do you think river snakes like swimming along tunnels?"

"I expect they love it," said Araminta, her teeth chattering. "It's probably their favourite outing. I expect they look forward to it all day. I expect..."

"Oh shut up," said Wanda crossly.

"Well stop asking horrible questions then."

Wanda and Araminta sat together in silence at the top of the pile of stones.

"Can't you do a spell or something?" asked Araminta.

"I only know the sleep spell, the custard spell and the blue orange juice spell," said Wanda, "Dad's not a powerful wizard at all, we can only do spells for fun."

"There's only one thing to do then," said Araminta.

"What's that?"

"Yell."

"Help, HELP, HELP!" they yelled.

Barry screeched to a halt outside the Miracle Mushroom Farm.

"In there, old chap," said Sir Horace who was turning his map around, trying to work out which way up it should be.

Barry did not particularly want to go to The Miracle Mushroom Farm, especially with Great Uncle Drac in the back of the van. "Are you sure?" he asked.

"That's the place. Clear as day now we're here. Remember it well. Entrance to the escape tunnel due south, south-west and then round that corner a bit," said Sir Horace decisively.

Barry drove into the yard of the mushroom farm as quietly as he could. The last person he wanted to see was Morris Miracle.

"OI!" yelled Morris Miracle, appearing from behind a mushroom shed. "I thought I told you I didn't want any more of those blinking bat droppings!"

"WHAT?" came an indignant voice from inside the back of the van.

Barry got out of the van and rushed around to help Sir Horace out. Morris Miracle stood rooted to the spot with his mouth wide open as Sir Horace unfolded himself and stood up shakily.

"Forward!" boomed Sir Horace,

and he and Barry set off towards the escape tunnel.

Morris Miracle recovered himself.

"Oi, you two, not so fast! Where do you think you're going to, a blooming fancy dress party? This is my land and I'm telling you to scarper!" He planted himself in front of Barry and Sir Horace.

Barry thought fast. "I've got something to show you," he said, "in the back of the van." He propelled Morris Miracle around to the back of the van and opened the doors.

"Good evening, Morris," said Great Uncle Drac with a menacing smile.

"What were you saying about blinking bat droppings?"

"Um...." gulped Morris Miracle.

Barry and Sir Horace disappeared fast. They hurried off to a mound of large rocks behind one of the mushroom sheds and Sir Horace rattled excitedly.

"This is it, no mistaking it. Where's the cave? Aha... behind this bush here. In you go, Barry."

Barry squeezed behind a rather prickly bush and found himself standing in a small dark cave with a strangly familiar smell about it. He held his nose.

"What now?" he called back.

Sir Horace followed him, looking at the map.

"Big hole two paces to the left."

Barry took two paces to the left.

"Can't see anything, Sir Horace, are you sure it's here?"

"Got to be, got to be," muttered Sir Horace. He clanked over to where the hole should have been. "Hey ho, what's all this?" Sir Horace kicked a pile of sacks.

"Someone's filled it in. Jolly bad luck, that. Castle rule number one: never fill in the escape tunnel."

Barry looked at the sacks.

"It's that Morris Miracle again," he exclaimed. "That's where he's put all of Drac's Organic Bat Fertiliser!"

"Right," muttered Barry. "It's worth a try..." He snapped his fingers and a sack flew straight out of the hole. Unfortunately it landed with a thud right on top of Sir Horace who collapsed in a heap on the floor.

"Oh my goodness, my spells never work properly," said Barry. "I'm so sorry..."

"Don't give it a thought, quite all right," mumbled Sir Horace from underneath his left leg. An armour-clad arm waved a piece of paper in Barry's direction.

"Here, take the map and get down that tunnel. Cross marks trapdoor. Through trapdoor to upper maze. Follow map. I'll wait for you here! Good luck, old boy! No time to lose!"

"Thanks," said Barry. He stood on the next layer of sacks and started throwing them out, wondering how many months Morris Miracle had been storing Drac's Organic Bat Fertiliser for.

Suddenly something moved under Barry's feet. The sack he was standing on disappeared from under him and he crashed down through the darkness.

"OUCH!" yelled Brenda, "Barry!"

"Ouch!" moaned Barry, "Brenda?"

CHAPTER TWELVE

"Barry!" exclaimed Great Aunt Tabitha. "What on earth are you doing here?"

"I could ask you the same question," groaned Barry, as Brenda helped him to his feet.

"We've been looking for Araminta and Wanda but we got turned back by the water and ended up here. We've got to find them quickly!" said Brenda.

"I know," said Barry. "Follow me."

"You know? How do you know?" asked Great Aunt Tabitha, hurrying after him.

"It's a long story," said Barry. "But I've got Sir Horace's map of the water maze here. The first thing we need to find is a trapdoor... then we can get into the upper part of the maze where the river doesn't reach. Then we'll have to see if we can get any further down and find the them. Come on, we must hurry..."

All three of them broke into a run, their torch beams jogging up and down, searching the floor of the tunnel for the trapdoor.

"Here we are!" said Barry suddenly.

Great Aunt Tabitha pulled open the trapdoor and a damp musty smell hit them. They scrambled down the stone steps into the upper water maze, stopped and looked around them.

"Phew..." breathed Barry. "There are so many tunnels to choose from. Where do we start?"

"Shhhh..." whispered Great Aunt Tabitha. "Listen, I'm sure I heard something!"

They all stopped. There was silence.

"I think I can hear water!" wailed Brenda.

Barry was desperately trying to follow the map. "Shhh, Brenda."

"Oh Barry, can't you tell where we are?" Brenda was getting upset.

"Let's try this way."

They went around a corner and came to a door. Great Aunt Tabitha put her ear to it.

"I'm sure I heard something," she said.

Brenda pushed open the door and rushed in.

"Oh, Barry, whatever's happened in here? Look at all these swords and spears. It's creepy!" she gasped.

"HELP!!"

"Barry! Where did that come from? That's Wanda, I know it is!"

Brenda looked around for Barry but he'd gone.

"Barry... Barry  where are you?"

"Hey," squeaked a small scared voice. "Dad?"

Araminta and Wanda looking up in amazement at the hole in the roof, saw a foot dangling down through it. The water was now up to their waists.

"How do you know it's your Dad?" asked Araminta.

"No one else has stars on their shoes! Hey, Dad! Dad!" shouted Wanda happily. "It's us, Dad!"

"OUCH! Oww! Oh... WANDA, ARAMINTA? Is that you! Brenda, Tabitha, we've found them, they're all right!"

Barry dropped down through the hole in the roof and landed in the water. Great Aunt Tabitha peered over the edge, with a huge, happy grin on her face.

"Araminta, what are you doing down there? You've got your socks soaking wet!"

"Sorry, Aunt Tabby," grinned Araminta sheepishly.

"Well, up you both come and let's get you back home safe and dry."

Barry lifted Wanda and Araminta up through the hole in the roof to Brenda and Great Aunt Tabitha who grabbed hold of them.

"Wow!" breathed Araminta as she looked back down into the dark cavern and the cold water rushing by. "We only just made it."

Barry scrambled back up through the hole in the roof and looked at his watch.

"We've been very lucky," he said quietly. "It's only twenty past seven. There are still ten more minutes to go before high tide. It would have been up to the roof by then."

"Can we watch it come up to the roof then, Dad?" asked Wanda.

"Certainly not," said Barry. "We're going home. Now where exactly are we?"

CHAPTER THIRTEEN

Sir Horace stretched himself awkwardly and picked up his left foot. He had been sitting in the cave listening to the hours striking on the nearby church clock. It was nearly midnight and Sir Horace was worried. He had managed to put most of himself back together again but, as usual, his left foot was giving him trouble. He was looking at it thoughtfully when five bedraggled figures stumbled out of the hole.

"Sir Horace!" said Araminta in a tired voice. "Oh, it's lovely to see you!" Araminta was carrying something heavy and rusty, which she hid behind some sacks before going over to Sir Horace and helping him to his feet, or rather, to his foot.

"Thanks for the map, Sir Horace," said Barry.

"Glad to see you all, old chap," said Sir Horace happily. "Glad it was of some help."

"It was," said Great Aunt Tabitha. "We just had a spot of bother finding the way back out again, didn't we Barry?"

"Never was very good at map reading," said Barry cheerfully, heading for the cave entrance. I'll go and get the van." Suddenly he stopped. "Oh my goodness! I've just remembered Drac and Morris Miracle. I left them together hours ago."

"You'll have to tell him now, Dad," said Wanda.

"I don't suppose he'll need telling," said Barry glumly.

"Need telling what?" asked Great Aunt Tabitha.

Barry told her and Brenda all about Morris Miracle cancelling the order for Drac's organic bat-poo.

"I've had an idea," said Araminta. "I had lots of time to think about it while we were all trying to find the way out. Why don't we start our own organic mushroom farm?"

"But where would we grow the mushrooms?" asked Barry.

"In the maze!" said Araminta excitedly.

"They'd drown," said Barry. "It's impossible."

"Not in the upper maze they wouldn't. It's lovely and damp there, perfect for mushrooms. They'd love it!"

"It's a great idea, Dad," agreed Wanda. "And there's all those sacks of fertiliser already there. We could call it Amazing Mushrooms, get it? Now all you've got to do is tell Great Uncle Drac!"

"We'll all tell him," said Great Aunt Tabitha. "I think he'll be pleased. He's never liked that Morris Miracle."

They all walked slowly towards Barry's van. Araminta was making quiet clanking noises and trying to stay well behind Sir Horace.

"I wish you'd leave that thing behind, Araminta," said Great Aunt Tabitha. "You've got enough junk at home as it is."

"Shhh!" whispered Araminta, as Barry opened the doors of the van.

Drac was fast asleep and snoring loudly. There was no sign of Morris Miracle anywhere. In the distance the church clock struck midnight.

"Happy Birthday, Sir Horace!" said Wanda. "Five hundred and forty today!"

Araminta slowly lifted up the heavy iron sword that she had dragged all the way from the room in the maze and carefully placed it in Sir Horace's rusty hands.

"Happy Birthday," she said shyly.

Sir Horace seemed to sway slightly.

"Oh, it's…" he faltered.

"It says H.C.S.G. on it," said Araminta.

"Yes, so it does. It's my old sword. Oh my goodness me! I feel most peculiar…" Sir Horace smiled. "Thank you, thank you very much."

"We found somewhere really nice to give you a surprise party, but I don't suppose we'll be allowed to now," said Wanda sadly. "It was a lovely little room with a mosaic…"

"A mosaic floor?" asked Sir Horace.

"Yes," said Wanda. "How did you know?"

"That's where you found my sword, was it? Got a hole in the floor, has it?"

"That's right," said Wanda and Araminta together.

"Well," said Sir Horace, "that *would* have been a surprise. Still remember escaping through that hole." Sir Horace seemed to shiver. "Cold water that was. Filled up the old armour pretty quickly. Not a place I'd like to see again."

"Oh dear," said Araminta and Wanda, rather crestfallen.

Sir Horace coughed in an embarrassed kind of way. "Very kind thought, um… but now you've given me my sword back I can forget about that room. Nothing of me left there now.

Best present I could ever have."

"I think we should still have a party," said Brenda. "A birthday party and a celebration rescue party. How about tomorrow at five o'clock in the hall?"

"Well, if you're sure..." said Sir Horace shyly. "I could bring my sword."

Araminta and Wanda squeezed into the back of the van with Great Aunt Tabitha and Brenda. Barry helped Sir Horace into the front seat and they set off for home.

On the way out of the farm, Barry thought he saw Morris Miracle hiding up a tree.

"I wonder if Araminta and Wanda

saw him?" he thought.

But Araminta and Wanda hadn't seen anything. They were already fast asleep wrapped up in Great Uncle Drac's blankets.